Postman Pat's
Safari

Story by **John Cunliffe**
Pictures by **Joan Hickson**

From the original Television designs by Ivor Wood

André Deutsch/Hippo Books

Published simultaneously in hardback by André
Deutsch Limited, 105-106 Great Russell Street, London
WC1B 3LJ and in paperback by Hippo Books, Scholastic
Publications Limited, 10 Earlham Street, London WC2H 9RX
in 1986

ISBN 0 233 97990 5 (hardback)
ISBN 0 590 70591 1 (paperback)

Made and printed in Belgium by Proost
Typeset in Souvenir by Keyline Graphics

Here comes Postman Pat in his red van.
He has stopped at the post office to
read a new notice.

"Hm," said Pat. "I mustn't miss that. I'll get my ticket today."

All the people of Greendale wanted to go on the trip.

Mrs. Goggins was very busy selling
tickets.

It seemed a long time to September 13.
The day was marked with a red ring on
every calendar in every kitchen in
Greendale.

Every morning, Katy and Tom Pottage
asked their mother, "Is it time for the
trip, yet?"
And every morning, Mrs. Pottage said,
"Not yet. It won't be long. Now stop
pestering me, and get off to school."

The day of the trip came at last.
They all waited for the coach by the old
pump in the village square.
Miss Hubbard was wearing her new
hat; it had three big curly feathers in it.
Granny Dryden was wearing her 'fur'
coat.
All the children had bags filled with
crisps, sweets, and fizzy drinks.

Miss Hubbard looked at her watch.

"That coach is late," she said.

Sam said, "No, it's here. Listen!"

Yes; now they could all hear it. It was the coach. Soon it came; slowly up the hill, slowly round the bend, slowly into the square.

"Hurrah!" the children cheered.

They all got in, with many a cry of,

"Come and sit by me!"

and,

"Can I sit at the front?"

and,

"Don't forget your bag!"

The door closed – whoooooosh – and they were off.

They went over the hills and down the
valley to Pencaster.
They went fast on the motorway.
They stopped for a drink and a visit to
the toilet.

Off they went again. Then they left the
motorway.
There were more hills and windy roads.
Katy said, "We're back home."
"No, this is Wales," said Pat. "Look,
there's a Welsh signpost."
No one could read it.

At last they were there.

"Please be back at the coach by five o'clock," said the Reverend Timms, and off they all went.

They had a lovely time. They saw
kangaroos, and deer, and peacocks,
and a tree full of monkeys. They had
pony rides, and they fed the ducks.
There were slides and swings for the
children.

Granny Dryden was the first one to find
the cafe, hidden amongst the trees.
"That was a lovely cup of tea," she
said.
A large bird flew down and pecked at
the feathers on Miss Hubbard's hat.
"Help!" she cried.
"Shooo! Go away! Shooo!" cried Pat,
flapping his arms at the bird. "It thinks
you're another bird, Miss Hubbard."

The bird would not go away. So Pat
took the feathers out of the hat, and put
them in his pocket.
"They'll be safe there," he said, "and
we can put them back on the coach."

"I think I like the hat better without feathers," said Miss Hubbard.
Then, when she had put on her hat, a monkey jumped out of the tree, and pulled it off again!

It ran up into the tree with the hat, then
sat on a branch where no one could
reach it. Poor Miss Hubbard!

Pat said, "We'll never catch it, now."

Then he had an idea.

"Don't move," he told Miss Hubbard.

"And keep your eye on the monkey."

He ran to the cafe, and bought a bag
of nuts.

He ran back to Miss Hubbard.

He threw a nut to the monkey.

It caught it in its mouth, and ate it.

Pat shook the bag of nuts at the
monkey.
"Come on! Come down for some more.
Lovely nuts!"

The monkey crept down the branch.
Pat threw some nuts on the ground.
The monkey jumped down, dropped
the hat, and began to nibble the nuts.
"Quick, Pat," said Sam. "Now!"

Pat crept up behind the monkey, and
grabbed the hat.

"Oh, thank you, Pat," said Miss
Hubbard.

"It's a bit dusty and bent," said Pat.

"It'll be all right when it's been to the
cleaners," said Miss Hubbard.

Later, when Granny Dryden was
sitting watching the peacocks, Tom
said,
"Look! Look, on Mrs. Dryden's fur
coat!"
A little grey monkey had curled up and
gone to sleep on her furry lap.
"It thinks you're its mum," said Pat.

When five o'clock came, the coach
driver tooted his horn to tell them it was
time to go home.
The children said, "Oh, can't we stay
longer?"

But most of them were asleep before the coach was on the motorway.

The coach broke down on the steep hill into Pencaster. And who do you think had a piece of wire and a pair of pliers in his pocket to help mend the engine? Ted Glen, of course.

They all said it was the best church outing ever.

Jess was asleep by the fire when they got home; but there were bits of straw and corn in his fur.

"I think Jess has been on safari in Alf Thompson's barn," said Pat.